SARAH FINAN

Erik
The Lone Wolf

Lincoln Children's

D0184140

Inspiring | Educating | Creating | Entertaining

Brimming with creative inspiration, how-to projects, and useful information to enrich your everyday life, Quarto Knows is a favourite destination for those pursuing their interests and passions. Visit our site and dig deeper with our books into your area of interest: Quarto Creates, Quarto Cooks, Quarto Homes, Quarto Lives, Quarto Drives, Quarto Explores, Quarto Gifts, or Quarto Kids.

Erik the Lone Wolf © 2018 Quarto Publishing plc. Text and illustrations © 2018 Sarah Finan.

First Published in hardback in 2018 by Lincoln Childrens.
This paperback edition published in 2018 by Lincoln Childrens, an imprint of The Quarto Group. The Old Brewery, 6 Blundell Street, London N7 9BH, United Kingdom. T (0)20 7700 6700 F (0)20 7700 8066 www.QuartoKnows.com

The right of Sarah Finan to be identified as the author and illustrator of this work has been asserted by them in accordance with the Copyright, Designs and Patents Act, 1988 (United Kingdom).

A catalogue record for this book is available from the British Library.

ISBN 978-1-78603-665-0

The illustrations were created with mixed media • Set in Grumble
Designed by Zoë Tucker • Edited by Jenny Broom • Production by Kate O'Riordan
Manufactured in Shenzhen, China RD112017

9 8 7 6 5 4 3 2 1

MIX
Paper from responsible sources
FSC® C017606

High in the mountains,
far, far away, lived Erik the wolf cub,
and the rest of the wolf pack.

The wolf pack did **everything** together...

which could be a bit frustrating for a young cub.

"**Erik!** Don't climb that high!"

"**Erik!** Hold your sister's paw!"

"Erik!
Don't go so fast!"

"Erik-"

"The mountains are full of danger.
That's why the pack always sticks together!"

Erik felt more and more crowded
by the pack and its silly rules.

Erik had had **enough.**

"That's it!" he muttered to himself.
"I'm going to be a lone wolf!"

And when no one was
looking, he walked away...

Further and further, until the wolf pack
was just a speck on the mountainside.

Now, there was nothing to stop
Erik from having **FUN!**

He climbed higher than he'd ever climbed.

He wobbled further than
he'd ever wobbled.

And he skied **faster** than he'd ever skied.

"I'm a lone wolf!" shouted Erik.
"Nothing can stop me now!"

Erik was right.

Nothing could stop him as he thundered down
the slope, too fast to read the sign that said...

DANGER!

It was too late...

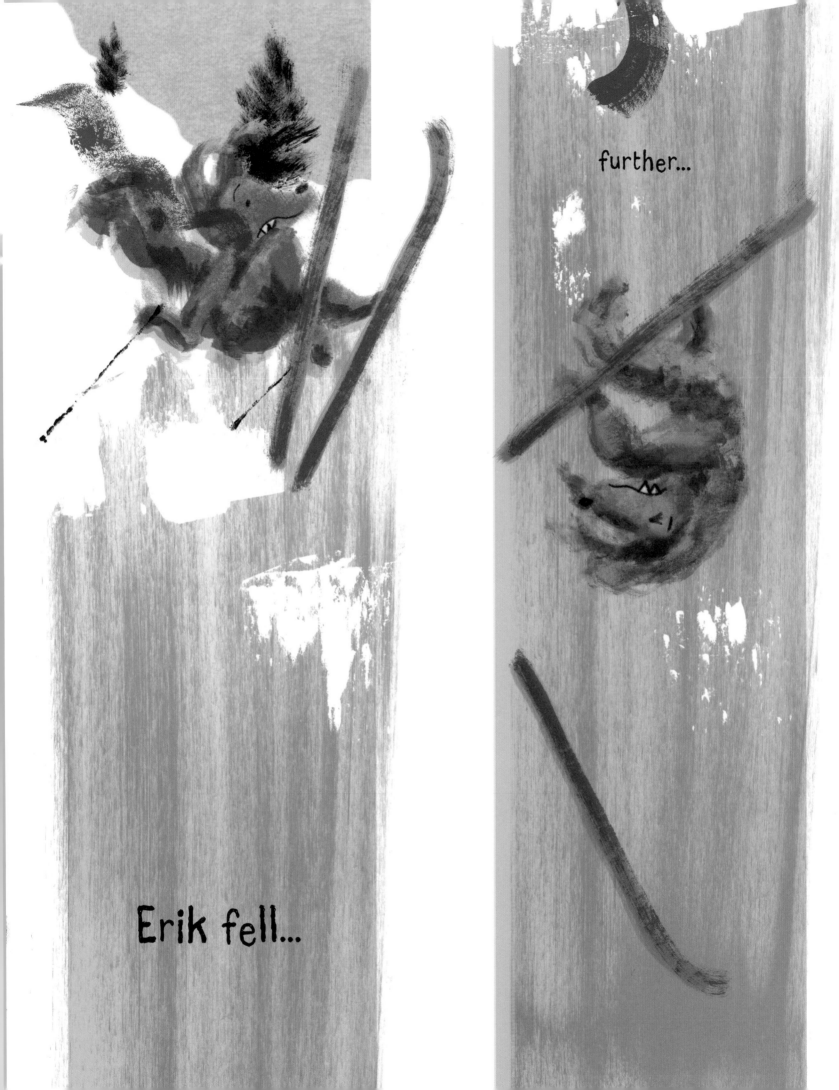

Erik fell...

further...

and further, until...

Oomph!

He landed far below,
at the very bottom
of the icy crevasse.

"Never mind," said Erik. "Lone wolves can get themselves out of trouble!"

But the ice was slippy...

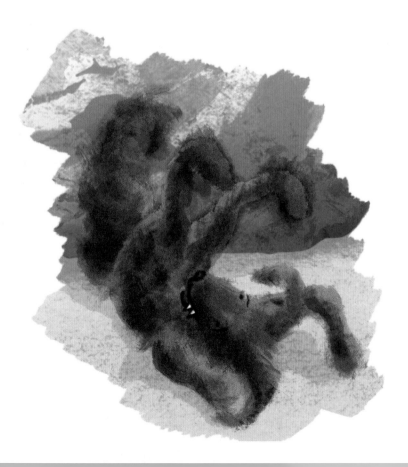

and the cliff walls were very high...

Even for a big wolf cub.

So he howled for help.

But Erik was all alone.

He waited...

and waited...

and waited.

As night began to fall,
Erik started to worry about
all the scary things that
might live in the mountains.

Then he heard a noise...

It was the wolf pack!

"Don't worry Erik," they called.
"We're coming!"

"**Erik!** Hold your sister's paw!" they shouted, lowering the smallest cub down into the crevasse.

Erik had never been happier to do as he was told.

Finally, back at the top, Erik found himself
in the middle of the pack's big, furry hug.

"The wolf pack always sticks
together!" they said.

"I'm not sure I want to be a lone wolf any more," whispered Erik that night. "Even big wolves need the pack sometimes," his family agreed.

After his adventure, Erik knew he'd never
feel crowded by the pack again.

Well, almost never!